DATE DUE			
MAY 3 04			

F
Er

Erickson, Jon E 1951

The steadfast tin
soldier

GUMDROP BOOKS - Bethany, Missouri

The Steadfast
Tin Soldier

QUALITY TIME™ CLASSICS

TALES
OF
HANS CHRISTIAN ANDERSEN

The Little Match Girl
The Steadfast Tin Soldier
The Top and the Ball
The Woman with the Eggs

Library of Congress Cataloging-in-Publication Data

Erickson, Jon E., 1951-
   The steadfast tin soldier.

   (Quality time classics)
   Adaptation of: Den Standhaftige tinsoldat.
   Summary: The perilous adventures of a toy soldier who loves a paper dancing girl culminate in tragedy for both of them.
   [1. Fairy tales. 2. Toys--Fiction] I. Andersen, H. C. (Hans Christian), 1805-1875. Standhaftige tinsoldat. II. Mogensen, Jan, ill. III. Title. IV. Series.
PZ8.E69St 1987 [Fic] 87-42582
ISBN 1-55532-345-6
ISBN 1-55532-320-0 (lib. bdg.)

This North American edition first published in 1987 by

Gareth Stevens, Inc.
7221 West Green Tree Road
Milwaukee, Wisconsin 53223, USA

First published as *Den Standhaftige Tinsoldat* with an original copyright by Mallings, Copenhagen.

Typeset by Web Tech, Inc., Milwaukee

2 3 4 5 6 7 8 9 92 91 90 89 88

The Steadfast Tin Soldier

by Hans Christian Andersen

retold by Jon Erickson

illustrations by Jan Mogensen

Gareth Stevens Publishing
Milwaukee

Once there were 25 tin soldiers, brothers all born from an old tin spoon.

"Tin soldiers!" were the first words they ever heard. They were said by a little boy on his birthday when he took the lid off their box.

He put them in a row on the table. They were all exactly alike — except for one, who had just one leg. But he stood as firmly on one leg as his brothers did on two.

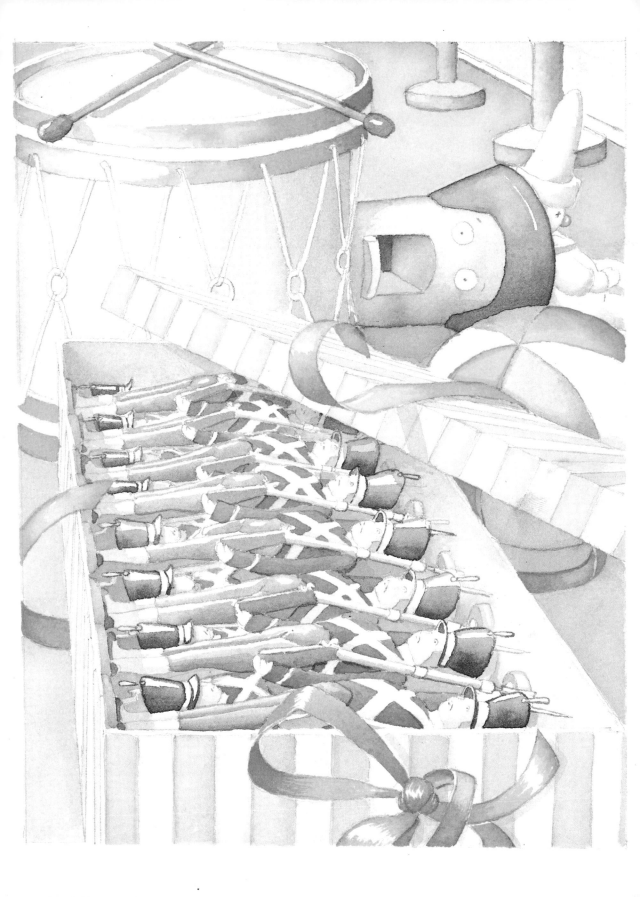

On the same table were many other toys. But the most wonderful was a cardboard castle. Before the castle were little trees around a mirror lake. This was all very pretty. But the prettiest of all was a little lady.

The lady was a dancer made of paper. She wore a tiny blue ribbon for a scarf, and around her neck hung a shiny spangle. She held her arms out wide and lifted one leg high behind her — so high the tin soldier could not see it. He thought she had just one leg — like him.

"She could be my wife!" thought the tin soldier. "But she is so rich and lives in a castle, while I live in a crowded box. But maybe if I got to know her..."

He lay where he could stay and look at her.

When night came all the other soldiers were
put back in the box. The people of the house
went to bed. Then all the toys began to play.
The tin soldiers rattled in the box, for they
wanted to play too.

The only two who did not move were the tin soldier and the little dancer. And he kept his eyes on her always.

The clock struck twelve. Suddenly the top flew off the jack-in-the-box next to the tin soldier. An evil troll popped out.

"Tin soldier!" he cried. "Keep your looks to yourself!"

The soldier pretended not to hear him.

"Just you wait until tomorrow!" snarled the troll.

The next morning the tin soldier was placed in the window. Whether it was the wind or the troll that did it, the window flew open and the soldier fell out and down into the street!

The maid and the little boy ran down to search. They almost stepped on him, but they couldn't see him.

What a frightening trip! The tin soldier had landed upside down with bayonet and helmet stuck between the stones in the street.

It began to rain hard. Streams raced through the streets. When it finally stopped, two boys came by, playing in the water.

"Look! A tin soldier! He can sail in our boat!" The boys put the soldier in their newspaper boat and sailed it in the water that ran down the gutter.

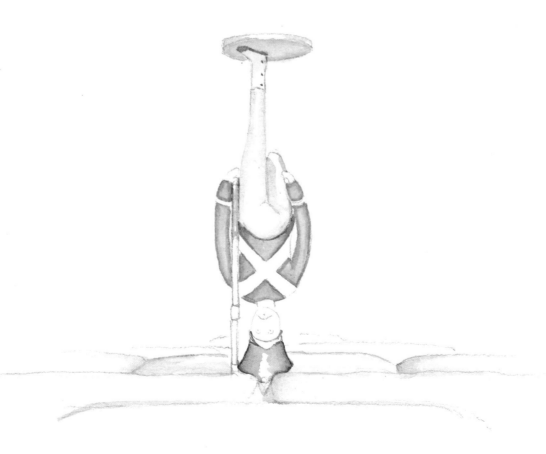

How fast the water ran! The paper boat
rocked up and down, sometimes spinning in
circles. The tin soldier trembled with fear.
But he remained steadfast, never moving,
staring straight ahead.

Suddenly the boat entered a drain, and it was
as dark as the box back home.

"Where to *now*?" thought the tin soldier. "I
know it's all the troll's fault. If only the little
lady could be with me right now, I wouldn't
care if it was twice as dark!"

A rat rose up before him and said, "Have you
got a passport?"

The tin soldier did not answer, but firmly
sailed on by. The rat swam after him
shouting, "Stop him! Stop him! He hasn't got a
passport!"

The rush of water grew stronger and stronger, carrying the tin soldier away from the rat. He saw light ahead. At the same time he heard a frightening roar. At the end of the tunnel the stream entered a great canal. The tin soldier was carried down the waterfall and out into the canal.

The soldier stood as stiffly as possible, while the boat whirled around and around. It began to fill with water.

The boat was sinking. The water was soon up to the soldier's neck. The paper began falling apart and the water closed over his head. He thought of the little dancer, and how he would never see her again. He remembered these lines from a poem:

Onward, onward warrior brave,
This course will take you to your grave.

The paper boat tore in half and the tin soldier fell right through. But just then a large fish swallowed him up.

How dark it was inside the fish! It was a very tight fit, too. But the tin soldier remained steadfast, still holding his rifle straight on his shoulder.

The fish darted crazily this way and that, and then became very still. Suddenly bright light appeared and he heard a voice say, "The tin soldier!" The fish had been caught and sold to the maid. She had cut it open with a knife! She gripped the tin soldier with two fingers and carried him into the next room, so that all could see the amazing man who had traveled inside a fish.

What a strange world! The tin soldier was
back on the same table in the same room he
had left.

There was the castle. And there was the
dancer.

She was still standing on one leg, as steadfast as he. This almost made the tin soldier cry tin tears, but this a soldier should not do. They looked at each other, but never said a word.

Suddenly one of the little boys took the tin soldier and threw him into the stove. There was no reason for this. The troll must have made him do it.

The tin soldier was lit up by the flames all around him. He felt very hot. But he didn't know if this was from love or from the fire. He still looked at the little dancer, and she looked at him.

He felt himself melting, but bravely he held steadfast. His rifle was still on his shoulder, and his eyes still on the dancer.

Someone opened a door and the wind blew the little dancer right into the stove where the tin soldier was. She burst into flames and was gone. The tin soldier melted away.

The next day, when the maid cleaned the stove, she found a little tin heart. This was all that was left of the tin soldier. All she found of the dancer was her spangle among the ashes. It was burned as black as coal.

THE END